This Little Tiger book belongs to:

STRATHDEVON
PRIMARY SCHOOL
Nursery Class

This book is presented to

Holly McFarlane

By Strathdevon Nursery
Christmas 2018

LITTLE TIGER PRESS LTD,
an imprint of the Little Tiger Group
1 Coda Studios, 189 Munster Road, London SW6 6AW
www.littletiger.co.uk

First published in Great Britain 2007
This edition published 2016

Text copyright © Claire Freedman 2007
Illustrations copyright © Gail Yerrill 2007
Claire Freedman and Gail Yerrill have asserted their rights
to be identified as the author and illustrator of this work
under the Copyright, Designs and Patents Act, 1988

A CIP catalogue record for this book is
available from the British Library

Printed in China
ISBN 978-1-84869-476-7
LTP/1900/2351/0718
2 4 6 8 10 9 7 5 3

The Magic of Christmas

Claire Freedman

Illustrated by

Gail Yerrill

LITTLE TIGER

LONDON

The mice are out gathering holly,
As soft snowflakes swirl everywhere.
There are hushed little whispers
of Christmas,
And a magical feel in the air.

Little Mouse shares the excitement,
As he scampers about in the snow.
But what is the magic of Christmas?
That's what he's longing to know!

"It's sitting indoors," says Grandpa,
"And letting the fire thaw your toes.
It's the warm smell of baking and spices,
Deliciously tickling your nose."

His brother squeaks, "Building a snowman,
    And patting the snow into place.
Then dressing him up in a hat and a scarf,
    With raisins and nuts for his face."

"It's going outdoors
to play snowballs,
And throwing them all, one by one.
It's running away to hide by a tree,
The best part of
Christmas is fun!"

"It's sledging downhill," laugh his cousins,
"To land in the soft, sparkling snow.
It's skating and sliding, out on the ice.
The magic is how fast we go!"

to little mouse

merry XM

His sister says, "Christmas means presents,
And smuggling them home, secretly,
To wrap up in bright, shiny paper,
With big love and kisses from me."

"It's soft voices singing,"
says Grandma,
"Sweet carols —
all through the night.
With little ones
huddled together,
Warmed by our
lantern's bright light."

"It's making our
own decorations,
From ribbon and paper and glue.
The magic's in sparkles and glitter,
And colourful
paperchains too!"

"It's hanging the tree lights," says Daddy.
"That twinkle and glow through the night.
It's pinning the star on top of the tree —
The magic of Christmas shines bright."

"At last it is Christmas!" smiles Mummy.
"We're together, in one happy house!
Sharing and feasting and opening gifts,
The magic is love, Little Mouse!"

Our long, happy day is now over,
The silvery moon starts to rise.
"Have you had fun?"
Mummy asks Little Mouse.
"It was magical!"
Little Mouse cries.

Mummy Mouse smiles
as she hugs him,
"The magic's in all that we do!
With loved ones and friends,
all together we share
A magic that lasts the
year through!"

More great stories from Little Tiger Press!

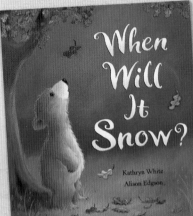

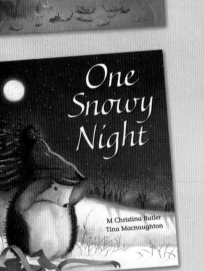